WHAT CAN YOU BE?

by Andy Rector

Illustrated by
Mary Lou Faltico

What will you be?
What will you be?

HALLOWEEN

is coming.

What will you be?

OCTOBER
1 2 3
4 5 6 7 8 9 10
11 12 13 14 15 16 17
18 19 20 21 22 23 24
25 26 27 28 29 30 31

Maybe a
GHOST!
You can float in the air.
You can say,
"BOO!"

Maybe a
WITCH!
You can ride on your broom.
You can make scary faces.

Maybe a
PIRATE!
You can carry a sword.
You can say,
"AHOY MATIE!"

Maybe a

KITTY!

You can purr.

You can say,

"MEOW."

Maybe a
COWBOY!
You can ride a horse.
You can swing a lasso!

Maybe a
PRINCESS!

You can wear a crown.

You can live in a palace.

Maybe an

ASTRONAUT!

You can ride a space
shuttle!
You can float in space!

Maybe a

CLOWN!

You can juggle.

You can make people

smile.

Maybe a
BEAR!
You can eat honey.
You can say,
"GROWL!"

Maybe a
SOLDIER!
You can march.
You can guard the palace.

HALLOWEEN

is coming.

What will you be?

–the end–